Monkey's Skateboard

Story by Annette Smith
Illustrations by Chantal Stewart

"Look at me!" shouted Monkey.

Monkey went up and down
and up and down
on his skateboard.

L.T.

"Little Teddy!" shouted Monkey.

"You can ride my skateboard."

"No," said Little Teddy.

"Your skateboard is too big

for me!"

L.T.

"I can ride your skateboard,"
said Rabbit.

"Look at Rabbit!" shouted Monkey.

L.T

"Come on, Little Teddy,"
said Monkey.

"No," said Little Teddy.
"I will stay here on my bike."

L.T.

Monkey looked at his skateboard.

He looked at
Little Teddy's bike.

"I can ride my skateboard
on the path," said Monkey.
"You can ride your bike
on the path."

"A race!" said Little Teddy.

L.T.

"Go!" shouted Rabbit.

Monkey and Little Teddy
went up and down the path.

L.T.

"Here I come!"

shouted Little Teddy.